Stranded
—at—
Plimoth
Plantation
—1626—

For Sylvia Spencer Kodjbanoff Keiser

Stranded
at
Plimoth Plantation
1626

words and woodcuts by
Gary Bowen

Introduction by David Freeman Hawke

HarperCollinsPublishers

Introduction

*T*wo days of a brutal winter storm that has left me housebound with nearly a foot of snow outside my study have helped me to appreciate anew the suffering endured by the Pilgrims when they landed at Plimoth on a frigid mid-December day in 1620 after eleven weeks at sea. They went ashore and thanked the "blessed God of Heaven" for having guided them over the "furious ocean," Governor William Bradford writes in his magnificent *History of Plimoth Plantation*.

Americans regard the Pilgrim immigrants with a special affection that has not diminished for nearly four centuries. They started out from "the mean townlet of Scrooby" in southern Yorkshire, England, where neighbors harassed them for being Separatists—a heretical sect that wished to break away from the state-controlled Church of England headed by the king and an often corrupt hierarchy of bishops. The Pilgrims-to-be left England for the more tolerant Holland. There they lived comfortably for eleven years, but other parts of their life in Holland did not please them. The Dutch view of Sunday as a day of pleasure disturbed these solemn, devout people, as did the growing use of the Dutch language among their children, who began marrying young Dutch people; a number of the children joined the army, others took to the sea, and some "worse courses." As the immigrants saw their English ways being diluted, they began to talk of crossing to America. And so they did.

Their early history in America was a catalogue of disasters. Nearly half the settlers died the first winter, and only six or seven remained healthy enough to tend the sick. John Carver, the first governor, died in May 1621; William Bradford succeeded him and led the colony for thirty-three years with a firm but compassionate hand. Elder William Brewster, who had attended Cambridge University and knew Latin plus a smattering of Greek, ministered to the settlers' souls. The Pilgrims were too poor to afford a paid preacher. Besides, because they were Separatists, few clerics wished to be associated with them.

One misfortune continued to plague the Pilgrims for a number of years. They had borrowed money from some English merchants to help finance their trip across the ocean. These gentlemen—who ventured only money, not their lives—treated the Pilgrims, in the words of one historian, "much as a loan shark treats a man in difficulties." Seven years passed before Plimoth was free of them.

Plimoth survived its own mistakes and the oppressions heaped upon it. Its settlers would make no great mark on American history, like the Puritans who settled in Boston in 1630. They were humble people, not reformers or missionaries, nor, like the Boston Puritans, eager to build "a city upon a hill." They wanted only to worship God as they thought He wished to be worshipped. By the time Gary Bowen's narrative begins, they could look with pride on what they had achieved. They were a group of plain people who had entered "upon an extremely rash adventure for which they were badly prepared, but came through to ultimate success." They had survived! The first permanent English settlement north of Virginia to do so.

—*David Freeman Hawke*
Madison, Connecticut

November 22, 1626

*T*he *Sparrowhawk*'s crew set sail October 12 from London in hopes of reaching Jamestown, Virginia. Amongst the 26 passengers, mostly Irish servants, were Masters Fells and Sibsey. I was indentured to Captain Sibsey by my unscrupulous uncle.

On November 6 our ship crashed in fog on what the captain told us was a New England shore. A few of us were injured in the wreck; fortunately everyone survived.

My knee was crushed by a heavy barrel when I tried to salvage this journal that Grandfather had given me. The first mate fashioned a splint so I could get about.

We were frightened, stranded without shelter. While drying the pages of my book in the sun, I cried as much as when Mother died.

By the third day we were bewildered as to our next course of action. Then a band of Indians found us. I was amazed when one of them stepped forward and, after making strange sounds, clearly said, "Plimoth." He knew enough English to ask if we wanted to go to Plimoth Plantation. We feasted with the Indians and gave them gifts, and they sent a messenger to the white man's colony to engage help for us.

The following evening under the full moon, Governor Bradford arrived by shallop with men bearing corn, and provisions to repair the ship.

We set about patching the *Sparrowhawk* with pitch, oakum, and spikes. The Governor departed to trade with Indians and our plan was to continue our voyage south as soon as our ship was seaworthy.

A severe storm caused our vessel to lose its moorings, dashing the ship against rocks until it was beyond repair.

On our tenth day here, we were transported to Plimoth and will remain here until a ship can sail us 700 miles south to Jamestown. My leg became too swollen to walk on, and I had to be lifted into the shallop.

The soldiers said New Plimoth was established on the site of an abandoned Indian village 35 miles north of where our ship wrecked. Within an eight-foot paling I saw a fort and 30 houses arranged neatly on streets, as in England.

Lodging has been found for each of us, and I am staying with the Elder William Brewster family. Their house has only one room and a fireplace, but there is a wooden floor that is warmer than the clay we had in London. The Elder says only gentry can afford such floors back home, due to the scarcity of timber.

Here trees are so abundant they are burned instead of coal for warmth, leaving the air pleasant to breathe.

Windows are made of oiled paper as glass panes are too expensive an import. It is always dark inside.

I feel welcome! A fine dinner was prepared in my honor and we all became acquainted. Elder Brewster, who is a Separatist, told me he had been imprisoned in England for his Puritan beliefs. After his release, the family moved to Holland where they felt less religious restraint. There a son, Johnathan, learned the trade of making silk ribbons.

The Brewsters were among the original Adventurers who came over on the *Mayflower* in 1620. Their family wanted religious freedom and a good living. Daughter Fear married Isaac Allerton last year and lives two houses away. Son Johnathan and his wife, Lucretia, live with their little boy nearby. Wrestling and Love, who have not taken wives yet, help their father, Master Brewster, with the farm. There is also a boy, Richard More, who was put to the Brewsters. He is my age.

The Brewsters say it was wrong for my uncle to have indentured me, and they agree I should have been allowed the apprenticeship offered at the print shop where my grandfather is employed. There I would be learning the skill of wood engraving.

Mistress Brewster suggested that I cut scenes on smoothed boards and press them onto the pages of this journal. That would occupy me while my leg heals. She gave me the quill and ink with which I am writing.

Richard is going to share his bed and coverlet until some can be made or borrowed for me.

The physician, Samuel Fuller, will examine my knee tomorrow.

November 23, 1626

Today, with a sharp knife Wrestling lent me, I cut an image of a turkey onto cherry-tree wood.

Mistress Brewster showed me how to thicken ink with soot and oil, and after spreading a thin layer of that mixture over the surface of the woodcut, I pressed the block onto this journal. I am pleased.

The physician says I may walk now, but he cautioned moderation.

*H*is Worship the Governor met at the fort this afternoon with all of us who crossed on the *Sparrowhawk*. He told us that 21 other ships have arrived in Plimoth in six years, and said it may be months before another anchors again. We are to earn our board by working for the families with whom we reside. Our labors are to be reported weekly to Captain Sibsey or Master Fells.

I am happy that Richard lives and works here, too. When he was six years old, he came over on the *Mayflower* with two brothers and a sister who did not survive their first year here. Richard says they had been told that their mother and father died, but he does not remember their illnesses or any funeral services. He says his parents did not like each other.

My knee aches and I am cold because my garments are not warm enough for this climate.

November 26, 1626

Squanto, the Indian who once saved the Adventurers' lives, visited our settlement this morning.

Johnathan told me that Squanto had been abducted in 1614 by the treacherous Captain Hunt to be sold as a slave in Spain. He escaped to London, where the authorities gave him passage back to Cape Cod.

When the *Mayflower* landed six years later, Squanto pleaded with his fellow warriors not to kill the settlers. He reminded them that one evil white man had stolen him, but many who were kind aided in his return. Squanto told his tribe that the newcomers were as helpless children in this country and should be shown how to survive here.

I am going to begin a likeness of Squanto after we eat. Ink must be stiffer!

November 28, 1626

Bear, John Goodman's mastiff dog, follows me everywhere. Love says one spaniel as well as cats were also brought over on the *Mayflower*. I miss my great white puppy, but Loyal, the Brewsters' dog, is a comfort.

Richard and I split and stacked wood all day.

My knee is so swollen this evening that the Mistress has insisted I rest it tomorrow.

I am going to follow Wrestling's suggestion and do a woodcut of this house. If it comes out well, I will press a print of it onto a blank page in the Elder's Bible and sign it for him.

Christopher Sears

This was court day for the plantation. Legal matters are judged on the first of every third month. The Governor presides and sometimes there is a jury. Since no barristers live in New Plimoth, the people must represent themselves.

The Elder, who attended court this afternoon, told us that Demaris Hopkins, who is six years old, was placed in another home. Neighbors feared that she was being spoiled by her parents who did not make their little girl work.

The Hopkinses have seven children and live in a two-room house, which is one of the largest dwellings here. There are no castles in Plimoth!

Lucretia and Johnathan are expecting a child in the spring.

The seafood is different from what we ate at home. Captain Sibsey loathes the lobsters and says, "Such crawly things are unfit for human consumption." I dare not record some of his other comments as I have been told never to write such words.

Mistress Brewster said we will be having pork soon. Our neighbors, the Billingtons, are

going to slaughter a pig that will be shared amongst several families.

I like the pumpkins and squash, which they say grow on trailing vines. If the seeds were available, they would probably grow in the gardens back home.

December 16, 1626

*T*he militia drilled today and it was Love's turn to participate. He marched and fired a musket with the others.

It has been cold and there was a light snowfall.

I never thought soap or candles would be luxuries, but they are imports here. There is not enough animal fat on the entire plantation to produce either successfully.

Lacking soap, it is difficult to get this ink off my fingers.

December 19, 1626

Drums summon us to worship after breakfast every Sabbath day. This was the fourth meeting I have attended since my arrival.

The service may be held in any location but due to the cold winter weather, the fort is being used.

There is preaching for an hour or two, followed by prayers, the Deacon's explanation, singing from the psalms, prophesying, almsgiving, and public discipline. Everyone is required by law to attend the eight-hour service, even though half the congregation are not Puritans.

Mistress Brewster enjoys the Sabbath because it is a day of thanksgiving and humiliation. Also, no labor, not even cooking, is allowed.

December 23, 1626

Governor Bradford talked with me today and showed me the notes that he has been keeping since he arrived in 1620. He commended me for recording my experiences here and said that I am participating in a "great event, which is the founding of God's community."

His Worship sug-
gested that I make
larger woodcuts and
consider using color.
The physician gave
me these mixtures.

December 25, 1626

*T*oday is Christmas but we did not celebrate at all, as the Puritans regard it as "a wanton papist holiday." I do not agree.

It is very cold inside.

We ate rabbit for dinner.

December 30, 1626

I was measured for new woolen breeches as my old ones are too small. The Mistress plans to sew them from fabric that once was her skirt. She will re-dye the cloth with agrimony roots and nutshells because all textiles are imported and difficult to come by here.

It is surprising that I have seen no spinning wheels or looms in Plimoth since they are so common in England.

This afternoon Goodwife Cooke stopped in to show her silk embroidered coif. She explained to me that the yarn produced by three to five people constantly at their spinning wheels could supply only one weaver's loom. No one can be spared from the fields to support the luxury of woven material as there is too much work to be done just to survive.

We had pork for dinner again.

January 6, 1626

*T*here was quite a ruckus today!

John Billington was placed in the stocks for fighting with his wife in the street. They had an argument because Elinor refused to wear a coif inside their house. Mistress Brewster says Elinor is very immodest to dress so improperly.

The Billingtons are not Puritans.

Love cut my hair quite short. I saw my reflection while visiting our neighbors. Master Hopkins has one of the only looking glasses in this settlement.

We ate a chewet pie made with raisins and dates. It was especially tasty.

January 16, 1626

*T*he Sabbath meeting seemed longer than usual and the fort was extremely cold. Richard fell asleep once, but I woke him so he was not clouted on the head by the Deaconess. He was very ashamed.

Eight inches of snow had fallen by the time the meeting was over.

Wrestling has a very bad toothache, and tomorrow the surgeon will relieve his pain. I will be occupied elsewhere at that time.

Lately I have not had time to do woodcuts. We all have been busy with just keeping warm.

January 20, 1626

*A*t thirteen years of age I am too young to be a regular member of the militia. Men 16 to 60 must take part in English-styled drills led by Captain Myles Standish, who is very short but mighty.

Even though Plimoth has never been attacked, the people are prepared to defend the plantation against privateers, who might pirate the stores of valuable beaver pelts. They also fear the Narragansett Indians, who live 45 miles away.

Trade agreements have been established with the neighboring Manamoyick tribe, which rescued the *Sparrowhawk* passengers and has always alerted the settlement of any dangers.

Fortnightly, a portion of the 75 members of the militia are drilled. Those who do not practice marching, loading, and firing muskets as scheduled are fined, put in the stocks, or whipped.

Bartholomew Allerton, Fear's stepson, is teaching me to beat a drum for the marching exercise.

January 23, 1626

*A*t today's meeting, the Deacon reminded us of our loved ones in England.

I wonder if my brother was sold as a servant, and if my grandparents know where I am.

Mother and Father should not have died. . . .

Master Brewster will include me in his tutoring of Richard, Oceanus Hopkins (who was born aboard the *Mayflower*), and Peregrine White, who Master Brewster says is the first Anglo-Saxon born in New England.

We had cold eel pie in a coffin for dinner.

January 28, 1626

*T*he birth of a girl child today was a joyous occasion to John and Elizabeth Howland. Mistresses Bridgett Fuller and Sarah Jenney acted as midwives. Fear served bread with ale to all the

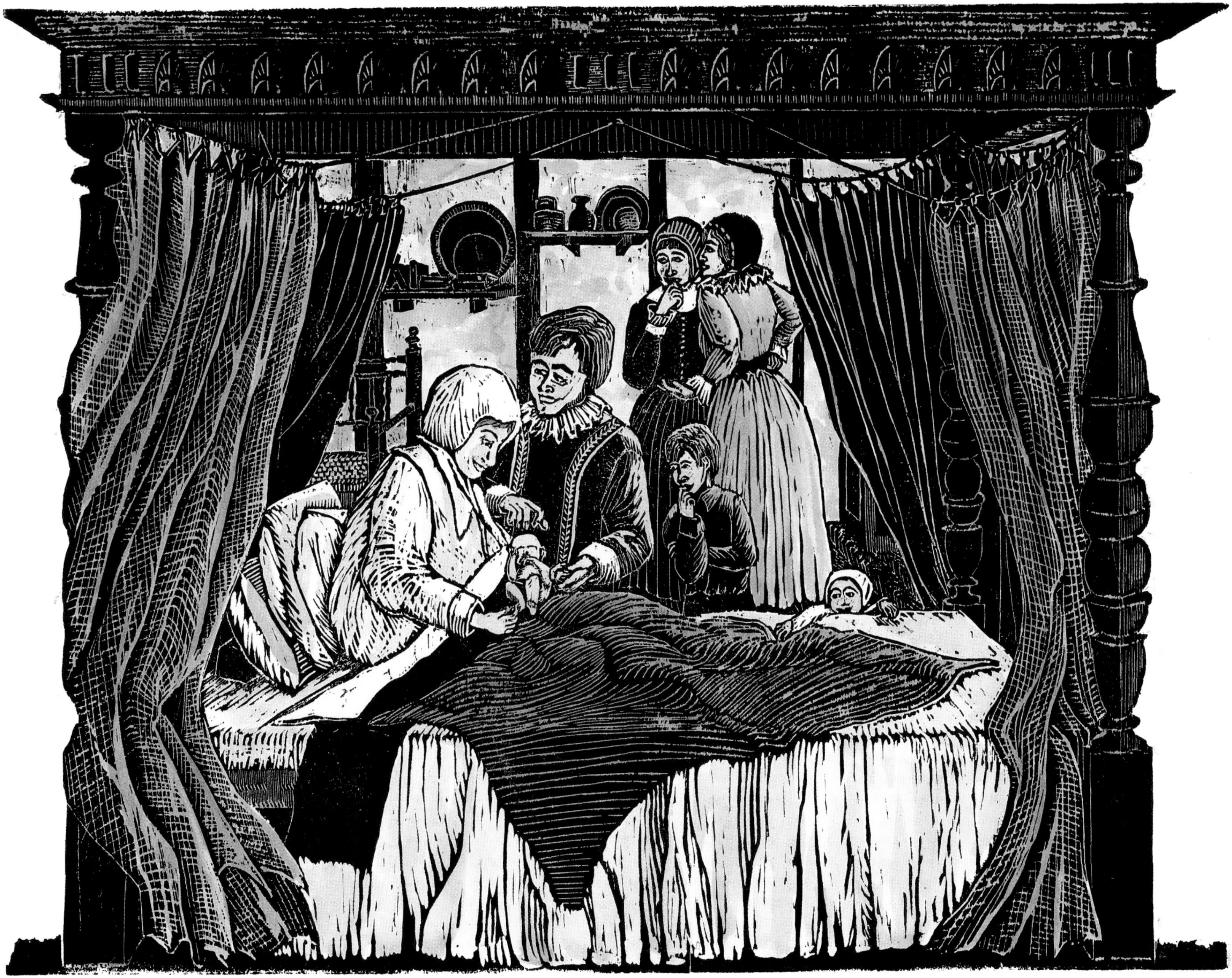

women who attended the borning.

The Howlands need to find a proper wet nurse for the infant as the midwives say that the character of the nurse is passed on through the milk. I wonder who nursed John Billington. . . .

Goodwife Elizabeth will not be out of bed for a few weeks, so Mistress Brewster is looking for a woman who is honest, not given to drinking, and willing to nurse the baby for one year. Best she be a Puritan!

February 3, 1626

I am happy that my schooling continues.

Each evening Master Brewster works with me on herb lore, farming, reading, and scriptures. He says the Plimoth people are more learned than in most English villages, as all parents must educate their children, even if that requires tutoring in another home.

The house is so cold and drafty this February night that the sap has frozen into icicles at the ends of the burning logs. Still we recited The Ainsworth Psalter to meter. Peregrine and Oceanus were excused from attending.

*T*his is Grandmother Hemphill's 66th birthday. I pray that she is well.

The Brewsters suggested that I send a message to my grandparents to notify them of my whereabouts as soon as a ship arrives to carry Plimoth exports to England.

Tomorrow I will be helping Master Peter Brown cut lumber for the house he plans to build next summer.

Mistress Brewster prepared Lombardy tarts—made with beets and melted cheese—for our evening meal.

*J*ohn Cooke was placed in the stocks for smoking tobacco in the street.

Johnathan showed me some of the silk ribbons he wove in Holland. Unfortunately there is not enough demand in Plimoth to support such a fine craft. He gave me a scarlet ribbon to mark my place in this diary.

We began constructing a roof on the fort today.

It is still very cold out.

February 17, 1626

*W*hen I was dressing this morning, by accident my shirt went on inside out. Elinor Adams, who was peering into the house through a crack in the wall, screamed at me not to reverse it. She said to wear it that way for it was a sign of good luck.

I am unaccustomed to this Puritan notion of constantly checking the wrongdoings of others.

Later this day I ripped my breeches and burned my thumb.

The night air is very cold.

February 24, 1626

*T*oday it was my turn to beat the drum for the militia. Captain Standish says my timing is precise and I am an asset to the company.

Richard and I stacked three cords of wood and split kindling. My knee aches.

The cattle ate greedily all day, so bad weather is sure to come.

We had roast pork and stuffed squash for dinner.

March 1, 1626

*T*his afternoon it seemed everyone rushed to the fort, because the court tried two of Master Fell's servants for stealing a wrought glass and running away.

Nanepashamet, an Indian, said he found the servants, Stephen Leicester and Kerrin Stinnings, 15 miles south and was offered the glass if he would not tell on them. The servants were returned to Master Fells by the Indian.

The trial proved that the glass was their own property and it had been given to them by Master Fells for their aid in salvaging the *Sparrowhawk*'s cargo.

Stephen and Kerrin are to be publicly shamed for deserting their master. Love said they could have been whipped for such a crime, but instead will be forced to wear halters.

Governor Bradford claims that there is less crime here than in England and that it is unnecessary to have a jail.

March 3, 1626

I was with a group of men organized by the Governor, cutting timbers in the forest.

Indians approached us, wanting to trade some furs, three turkeys, and a deer for grain. His Worship agreed to the barter, and the Indians will receive a bushel of corn.

If our muskets were more accurate, we would not have to rely upon the Indians for occasional venison and turkey.

Johnathan says the settlers are not good at hunting, and he thinks it is due to the King's declaration prohibiting hunting throughout England's forests.

A native took Resolved White and me aside to warn us of a trap he had set. One of our people had been snared once, and the Indians do not wish such an accident to happen again.

The Mistress predicts it will be warm tomorrow and all the snow will melt.

I am tired.

March 10, 1626

Manases Kempton and the widow Juliana Morton signed a betrothal contract today. If Manases decides not to marry her, he will have to go before the court for punishment. Johnathan says Manases is mostly interested in Juliana's dowry of woolen blankets, pots, pans, trenchers, and pewter chargers. Also there are chickens, swine, two she-goats, plus a house with six acres of land and five working-age children.

Johnathan thinks it is best to marry someone because you love them.

We had freshwater eels for dinner. They are in season all this month and are caught in special traps.

March 17, 1626

*T*rading has begun with the Abenaki Indians, who arrived wearing beaver pelts as coats. A pound of beaver is worth three shillings or a bushel of either Indian corn, oats, wheat, or barley. The beaver pelts are Plimoth's most valuable export and are used for making felt hats. I wish I had a good hat.

Mistress Brewster prepared a delicious pumpkin pie in a coffin. We also had squirrel stew.

I will send my grandfather some seeds for squash, pumpkin, and Indian corn, so he can start growing them back home.

March 25, 1627: New Year's Day!

I boarded the shallop for my first fishing trip and caught cod and hake.

Master Alden said that three years ago the plantation gave up exporting fish to England because they were not good enough at it to compete with the English seafood market. He is one of Plimoth's coopers, and he makes barrels for the freshwater eels, which are now pickled for England.

I have learned how to mend a fishing net, with hemp twine and a shuttle shaped like an arrow. I also know the seasons when each type of fish can be caught. In the months ahead, we will catch bass, bluefish, smelt, herring, pollack, and mackerel.

I was not seasick.

March 28, 1627

*M*istress Brewster says we will have to plant more carrots and beets this summer as last season's supply is almost depleted and what remains is withering.

I marched with my drum for the militia, and afterward Love let me help clean the musket he fired during the exercise. John Billington did not attend the drill and for that he will be punished.

Bartholomew and I had a fight after he broke my drumstick. We will probably be shamed at the next Sabbath meeting.

March 31, 1627

I enjoy the smells at the bakeoven. The men built it last year for the community's use, and in it can be baked 20 loaves of bread at once. It has a wattle frame covered with three layers of daub and looks similar to those which some bakers in London mount upon wheelbarrows to peddle their services through the streets.

The Plimoth oven does not hold heat well and is useless during the cold winter months.

Goody Billington fired it today as there

has been a break in the weather. She made six loaves of one-third bread, which has equal parts of wheat, rye, and Indian corn flours.

Everyone misses the grist mills for the convenience of purchasing fine flour. Here we grind by hand what in England would be considered coarse meal.

Tomorrow, Fear is going to use the bakeoven to make breads for her household and ours—that is, if the warm spell lingers.

April 5, 1627

I carried in 24 buckets of springwater to heat. Each member of the Brewster household had a bath today. It felt good to wash.

Love cautioned me that it is unhealthy to have more than three or four baths a year because, if

done too often, all the body's natural protection against disease is washed away.

Tomorrow we will be fishing for herring, which is plentiful this month and next.

April 7, 1627

Mistress Brewster is ill. Master Samuel Fuller, the surgeon, was called in to let her blood. He diagnosed her ailment as a case of overeating.

Master Fuller has promised to show me how to cast pewter spoons using his bronze mold.

We split and stacked more wood this afternoon.

I helped Love prepare clam stew. It was not good.

April 11, 1627

The Mistress is still not well. The surgeon is treating her humors with syrup of horehound, which he says should relieve the congestion in her lungs.

Elder Brewster is very worried about his wife's health.

Fear has been doing much of the cooking for us.

April 15, 1627

*T*his is the ninth day of the Mistress's illness, and her symptoms are more severe. She has a sharp fever and has been spitting blood.

Master Fuller thinks it is peri-pneumonia as her nose is crooked, eyes swollen, tongue dry, and her fingernails gnarled and black.

Conserve of violets has not helped, so Elinor Adams says repeating "abracadabra" to her will lessen the fever. I think that could be superstition. I am saying silent prayers.

April 16, 1627

A blessed event has happened!

This afternoon, Lucretia gave birth to a beautiful girl child that she and Johnathan have named Mary, after Mistress Brewster.

The Master hopes that the arrival of a granddaughter will aid his wife's recovery, as the Mistress seemed to respond with pleasure at the sight of little Mary.

Fear preserved our catch of mackerel by salting and hanging them in sunshine to dry. It was

an abundant catch, one that Mistress Brewster would have enjoyed!

Soon she will, I am certain.

April 17, 1627

When I awoke this morning, Master Brewster told me the Mistress had died in the night. I cannot write more.

April 18, 1627

As I helped Johnathan make his mother's coffin, he told me that half the Adventurers died their first winter here, due to the same illness suffered by Mistress Brewster. The disease is known as "the general sickness."

Johnathan says that because of their Separatist belief, death is not feared and services are very simple and without ritual.

When we finished the casket, the Mistress's body was covered with a wool shroud and placed in the box with rosemary for remembrance.

I shall never forget her.

April 22, 1627

*T*he funeral was held this day. Four of the women who respected Mistress Brewster carried her coffin to the graveyard.

A few neighbors gathered with the family and Deacon Fuller. We all stood reverently and quietly while earth and rosemary were placed on the pine box.

Warmed wine and confections were served at our house after the service.

I miss her. Since the death of my mother, no one has loved me as much as Mistress Brewster.

I have taken on extra chores. Goody Billington was upset when she saw me milking Red, our cow. Goody said I was doing woman's work. She also insists that I never again drink raw milk, as it should be consumed only as butter or cheese. I thought the fresh milk tasted good.

Temporarily, Richard's and my schooling has stopped. Master Brewster says his mind wanders and he cannot concentrate.

The house seems very empty. Loyal lies in a corner all day looking at the door expectantly. Poor dog does not understand that his mistress will never return.

April 30, 1627

*E*lder Brewster wants me to do some work for the Billingtons in exchange for Goody Billington milking our cow and occasionally cooking for us. She is not as good a cook as Mistress Brewster but better than Love or I.

Elder Brewster is lonely and cheerless. Wrestling does not sleep well at night. Tomorrow Richard and I will put our beds out on the fence to air in the sun.

May 5, 1627

I marched with the militia. During the drill, a musket accidentally fired, and John Billington cried out in agony as he fell to the ground. We thought John had been shot until he burst forth with laughter! Captain Standish was very upset and will use the stocks to punish unruly John.

I split a cord of firewood and am tired tonight.

We had chicken and the last of the carrots for dinner. Goody sent over some burned biscuits.

May 10, 1627

*L*ove confides he is thinking about marrying but has not said who he wishes to betroth. Elder Brewster seems delighted at this idea.

I am in no hurry to wed.

Richard and I helped with the smelt fishing. Using large bowls we scooped up the fish onto the shore by the hundreds. They are especially tasty cooked in a little butter.

The trees around the paling are budded, and there are some green leaves appearing.

The weather is warm and the air sweet.

May 11, 1627

*S*ome think an alehouse is needed here for entertainment. We do have spontaneous street dances despite the tiring endless work.

I remember the Plimoth settlers were shocked when Captain Sibsey danced with a woman. He insisted it was now the acceptable style of dancing in England.

But the Governor does not believe King Charles would approve of such a display. The Governor still insists that "men should dance with men and women with women, according to tradition, and anything different is disgraceful."

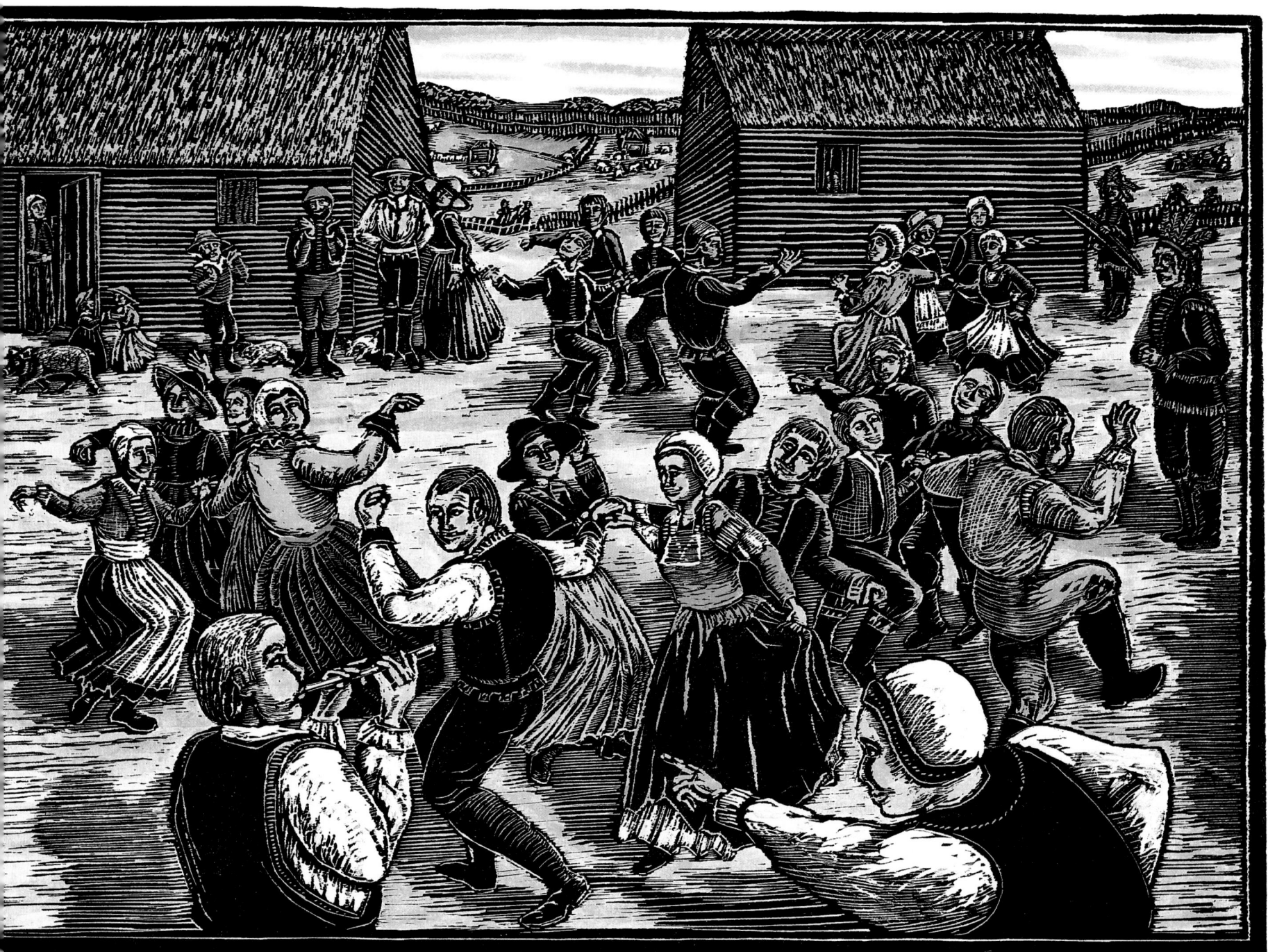

Most of the settlers are adjusting to seeing the *Sparrowhawk* passengers dancing together, but when John Billington tried a turn with Elinor, she boxed his ears.

My evening lessons have resumed with Master Brewster, and we will be concentrating on farming and barter.

May 12, 1627

John Billington is making cedar weatherboards to finish siding his house. Last fall it took ten men nearly a week to raise his house from timbers cut the previous winter. The roof was thatched in one month with Norfolk reeds, which the women gathered by the river.

John has taught me to make weatherboards using a froe. He is also going to show me how clapboards are riven from oak for the manufacture of barrels, this plantation's second largest export.

We had a good venison meal with Fear and her family.

I am going to learn how to play a flute that was brought over on the *Sparrowhawk*. The cargo also included bagpipes, recorders, lutes, citterns, and gitterns, none of which existed at this settlement until our ship's arrival.

Goody Billington and Mistress Cooke are wattling and daubing the interior walls of Goody's house. They weave branches and then cover them with a mixture of wet clay, sand, and straw.

John Billington has put bars in each window to keep out birds, which he says are spies for the devil. Goody hangs pottery in their chimney to keep out witches. Elder Brewster does not want me to cultivate their beliefs and says I am not to allow Goody to predict my future with her sieve.

It would be comforting to know if I will ever return to London. . . .

May 16, 1627

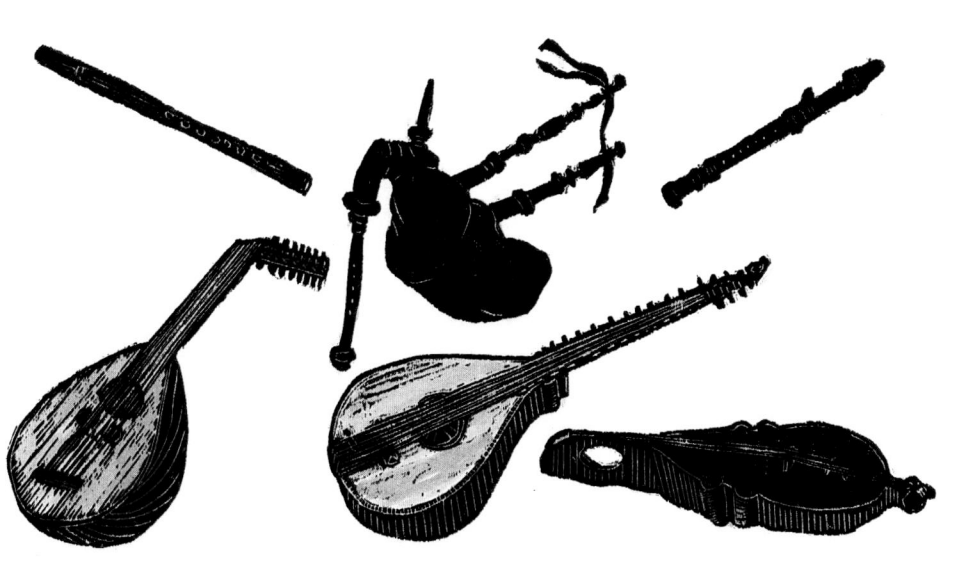

Since our animals were licking their hooves all day, we were not surprised when high winds brought a sudden storm that collapsed the Allertons' chicken house.

Elinor Adams says if you knock on a chicken house at midnight, the fowl will answer whether or not you

will marry within the year. If the cock crows before the hen clucks, a marriage is in sight.

Love refuses to rap on our chicken house. Sometimes he is too serious.

Tomorrow the widow Juliana Morton is going to marry Manases Kempton. Since it is her second marriage, a simple service will be performed with the couple speaking their vows before the Governor.

The days have been sunny and warm.

May 17, 1627

*M*aster Francis Eaton had me mend the fence around his garden. The livestock is allowed to wander within the paling so a sturdy barrier is necessary to keep the vegetables protected.

Goodwife Eaton plants cowcumbers, carrots, beets, parsnips, onions, and Jerusalem artichokes, plus turnips, radishes, lettuce, cabbage, and cauliflower. The Goodwife preserves cabbages by hanging them inside the house, and carrots by burying them in sand through the winter.

Resolved White and I dug clams along the beach and had a splashing contest that no one saw.

*A*lthough it has been a wet spring with much rain, the 200 acres of fields around the village have dried sufficiently to make tilling possible. Every man, woman, and child has been working on the acre alotted each family member according to the land division of 1623. The passengers of the *Sparrowhawk* have also been given land to work, so we can plant corn to earn our passage to Jamestown.

I do not wish to move.

May 21, 1627

I have been turning soil with a spade for the Brewsters' garden as well as working in the plot directed by Captain Sibsey. A cow is now used to drag the harrow, but I understand that before cattle were shipped over from England three years ago, the men and women did the pulling.

My hands are blistered and my skin is badly burned by the sun.

Tomorrow we will be doing more of the same field work.

*M*aster Brewster and Johnathan attended an important meeting concerning the division of the cattle. They said the plantation has been divided into 12 groups with 13 members in each group.

I believe our dinner of pork was tainted and now my stomach is upset. Love says if I do not feel well tomorrow, my blood will be let.

May 24, 1627

*R*emember Allerton gave me a shell on a string. I brought her some of the red flowers that are blooming near the south gate. Wrestling said these were picked from a poisonous plant that would make Remember's nose grow long and pointed overnight. I will pick Wrestling a bouquet tomorrow!

We had a fine dinner of mackerel stuffed with oysters.

*T*his morning a ship, the *Marmaduke*, arrived from London without passengers. The crew members had been sailing for nine weeks and did not look well as they came ashore.

Some were astonished at the primitive life-style we are living. One asked where the nearest cathedral was. This brought peals of laughter from most of Plimoth's residents.

Letters were passed out and we were informed of current events in England and King Charles's interest in further expanding the settlement of America. We found out that a ship's crew returning from Jamestown told our relatives back home that the *Sparrowhawk* had never arrived and was believed lost at sea. Memorial services had been held by some families for their lost loved ones.

The *Marmaduke* is going to return to England soon. Captain Sibsey and Master Fells are trying to convince John Gibbs, the ship's captain, to sail the *Sparrowhawk* passengers to Jamestown. No decision has yet been made.

May 27, 1627

*T*he sailors are staying in various households and were treated to a venison meal.

The Governor would like the ship to take us to Jamestown. Tomorrow His Worship is going to have a meeting with Gibbs to decide our future.

May 28, 1627

*C*aptain Gibbs has been trading soaps and candles in exchange for pickled eels, a British delicacy. Candles and soap are so precious to our settlement that they are priced high. There has been much trading for textiles, pottery, paper, and boots, all much in demand here.

The sailors wanted to see some Indians. I showed one the illustrations in this journal. He was sufficiently impressed.

I am waiting up for hours for Master Brewster to return with news from the meeting.

He said that the Governor pleaded a strong case as to why the *Sparrowhawk* passengers should be fared to Jamestown and that his reasoning was difficult to argue, especially since the welfare of so many people is concerned. But Captain Gibbs wants more time to decide and feels that he must consider his crewmen who were hired only to go to Plimoth.

I helped Master Stephen Hopkins carry several wonderful new pieces of furniture from the ship to his home. Master Hopkins was a wool merchant in London and debts were owed him when he moved to Plimoth. Since money is relatively unimportant here, he is paid with painted furniture.

Despite the dreary weather, we worked very hard today.

May 29, 1627

The ship is being repaired now. Rough seas caused it to spring several leaks, but they are easily patched. Captain Sibsey says that it is a sound vessel because it has a "cod's head and a mackerel's tail."

Everyone is preparing goods for export.

Even if the ship sails to Jamestown it will still carry the plantation's products back to England.

The sailors are concerned about the south wind being bad to breathe. Johnathan says that in London the air is so fouled by the river Thames that people do not have windows on the south side of their homes. Here we do not have windows facing south either, which must be an unnecessary custom that has continued.

Love and I have been stacking wood.

I do not sleep well and have had bad dreams about moving to Virginia, where the Indians are said to be very unfriendly.

May 30, 1627

Captain Sibsey appeared this morning to inform me that the ship will not be going to Jamestown and that I am to help load the cargo that will be exported to England. He then dashed off to notify the other *Sparrowhawk* passengers.

All day I had to pack dried herring, sassafras, pickled eels, and clapboards onto the ship.

Afterward, Master Brewster and the Governor were discussing the value of the beaver pelts, which will be loaded on board first thing tomorrow. They said that the furs should sell for 20 shillings per pound. The value of this year's fur trade with the Indians is about 1800 monetary pounds, enough to build over 400 homes. The fur is really the plantation's gold.

May 31, 1627

The *Marmaduke* set sail carrying one passenger, Isaac Allerton, who has business to take care of in London. Fear will miss her husband very much. Isaac has promised to deliver letters for me: one to my grandparents and a second to my aunt Ruth and uncle Willard, who also are concerned for my welfare.

I felt so relieved once the ship departed. Richard and I got everyone dancing!

June 1, 1627

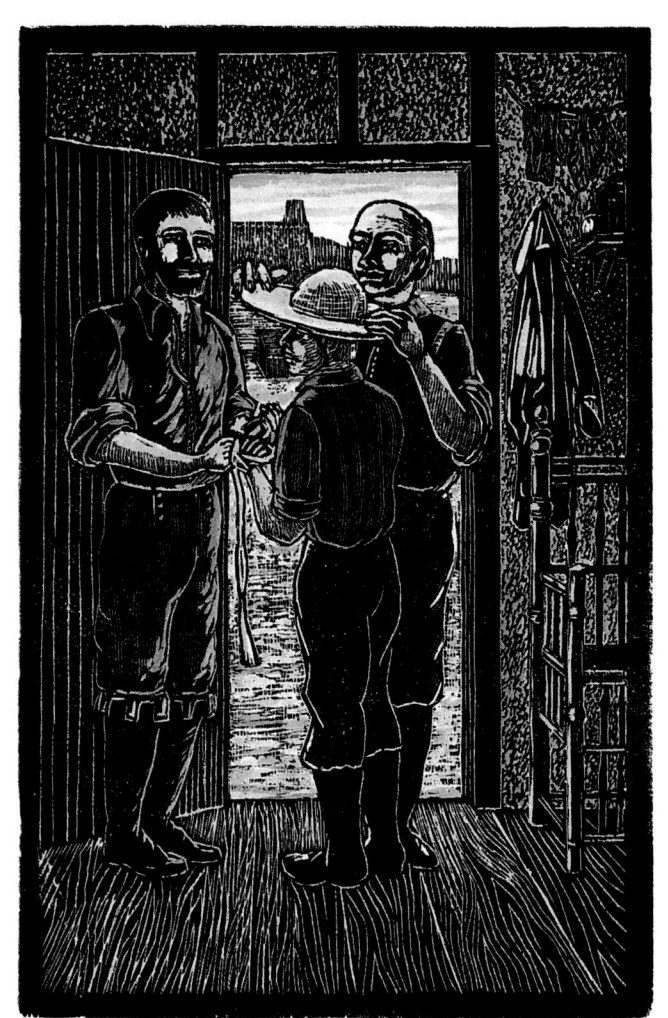

The Governor announced that today's scheduled court proceedings will be held on the sixth day of the month.

Because Master Brewster predicts rainy weather is coming, we worked doubly hard to sow our seeds for peas, beans, wheat, rye, barley, and turkey corn. Not all families have planted their crops yet.

Mistress Priscilla Alden gave birth to baby John. Master John Alden, her husband, was very pleased.

Love prepared mussels again.

June 2, 1627

Elder Brewster presented me with his late wife's prized beaver hat, and the fit is perfect. Love says his mother would be pleased to know that I will wear it. We added a new silk hat band—one which Johnathan wove in Holland years ago.

Rain has poured continuously for three days, and the night air is cool. If there are showers again tomorrow, my new hat will keep me dry.

June 6, 1627

I was a witness in court today. A property damage suit was brought against Manases Kempton, whose pig uprooted the Brewster garden and broke several of our pans.

After the bill of complaint was read, Manases was called to the stand and sworn in, and he said the whole matter was "oonty-toomps," which confused the court.

The Governor asked Kempton to explain himself but he kept repeating the unfamiliar word. Myles Standish told us "oonty-toomps" was a country term from the region of Colchester, where Master Kempton once resided. It means *molehill*!

Everyone in the courtroom burst into laughter except for the Governor, who was upset that Manases thought the court engaged in trifles. Kempton was found guilty of neglecting his beast and fined ten shillings due the plaintiff, as well as two shillings due the court for the disturbance of the King's Peace.

June 8, 1627

...d I worked with Master Brewster on our lessons. After our session, Governor Brad-...came by to discuss the construction of a trading post. Plans are now being drawn up for the structure.

Mistress Warren baked some delicious bread and brought us two loaves because I had cut and split wood to fire the bakeoven for her.

Richard and I will be weeding in the fields tomorrow.

June 10, 1627

I marched with the militia. Captain Standish made us repeat our exercises as he said we were not at our best. The heavy rains did not help our performance.

I hope Master Brewster will remarry. Johnathan says most people who are widowed wed again about one year after the death of their spouse.

Today marks the Master's sixtieth birthday. Fear stuffed and roasted a turkey. Johnathan, Wrestling, and Love had strong drink and were very silly.

June 12, 1627

*W*e reseeded the beans that had rotted in the ground due to excessive rains followed by cool temperatures. Other families had the same problem. The newly planted beans had better grow because seeds are scarce now.

Fear thinks she is in the family way. Elder Brewster seems happy that he may become a grandparent again. He recommends that every couple have "at least ten children to help establish a good farm and to lessen the work load for the parents."

I would not like living in a small house with a large family, as is customary here.

Goody Billington brought us some of her horsebread, made with peas and beans. It was tough chewing.

June 15, 1627

*D*aily I must account for the cow, sheep, and goats that are in the pasture. All summer the hogs will roam freely outside the paling, eating mussels, acorns, and beechnuts. I am thankful that the fowl—chickens, ducks, and geese—find their own food.

Master Nicholas Snow's dog had eight pups. Elder Brewster says we do not need another animal to feed and that Loyal is enough dog for this household.

His Worship the Governor has asked me to do an illustration of the proposed trading post. He wants my composition to depict the structure as if it were already standing on its site. The Governor says my "artistic ability should be revered and nurtured as it is a gift from God." My purpose in life could be unfulfilled, he says, if I "were to perform only menial labors."

The Governor is a very wise man.

June 17, 1627

Nathaniel Morton and I found strawberries outside the paling. His mother made them into conserve and gave me a portion for Elder Brewster to sample.

I picked our first lettuce and radishes and found them sweet and delicious.

When Wrestling and I were in the forest cutting trees we saw a giant bird that he called an eagle.

June 18, 1627

We worshipped on the top of the hill near the burial ground today. The Deacon's explanation concerned life after death. It was interesting.

He also reminded us that there are many more settlers buried here than there are markers. The graves were not marked the first years after establishing the settlement, to keep the Indians from knowing how weak in numbers the plantation had become.

Loyal and another dog were making nuisances of themselves during services, and I was asked to escort them home.

Our crops are growing rapidly and tomorrow I will be working in the field assigned to the *Sparrowhawk*.

June 24, 1627

I asked Master Brewster if there is any way that I may stay here to live and not go to Jamestown when a ship comes. He is going to discuss the matter with Captain Sibsey.

Love's clam chowder was tasteless again so I added my own spices.

The women fashioned garlands of flowers in preparation for tomorrow's nuptials.

One could not help but hear Elinor Adams loudly singing:

"Sundays for weddings,
Mondays for wealth,
Tuesdays for health,
Wednesdays best days of all,
Thursdays for losses,
Fridays for crosses,
And Saturdays, no luck at all!"

I think Elinor was in her cups. Every hour she was shouting, "Blessed is the bride on whom the sun doth shine!"

Johnathan said the Billingtons were married at midnight during a thunderstorm. I never should have asked Goody Billington if the information was true. My ears will be sore for a week!

June 25, 1627

Most everyone knew Jane Cooke would marry Experience Mitchell. It seemed especially certain after Jane found a pea pod with nine peas in it, placed it over her doorway, and had Experience as her first caller.

Their wedding was a festive occasion with a civil service performed by the Governor. The bride wore flowers in her hair and a wool lover's knot bound around the waist of a dress that she herself had refurbished.

The path of the bride and groom was strewn with rosemary and flowers. Wheat was tossed for fertility and the traditional loaf of bread was broken above Jane's head. "Bride's ale" was sold and we danced into the evening.

The couple received gifts of a looking glass, a small chest, and several pots of butter.

At the end of the day's celebration, all the single people escorted the newlyweds to Experience's home, where the bedchamber had been draped with even more garlands.

The couple was put to bed after their socks were removed. Then the single people took turns sitting at the foot of the bed, where each could toss a sock over his or her shoulder in hopes that it would land on the face of the bride. Anyone successful at this will be married within a year.

Jane was laughing so hard by the time Love's turn came up that the sock he tossed landed in her mouth. This was high merriment!!

June 29, 1627

Our cow was missing this morning, so Richard and I went on a search. By noon we had found her near a cherry tree laden with fruit. We picked our hats full and brought them home.

It occurred to me while watching Lydia and Phoebe Hicks preparing peas that the superstition about finding nine of them in a pod gets the shelling done faster.

We also shelled our peas for drying.

July 1, 1627

The weather has been hot and dry and our garden has suffered. Richard and I carried buckets of water to give the crops a drink.

Since there is no rain in sight, we plan to cut a field of grain tomorrow. After it is turned over to dry thoroughly in the sun, we will stack the barley in the shape of cones.

I boiled down seawater to replenish the Brewsters' salt supply.

Love says I am growing like a weed!

July 3, 1627

I have learned how to make spars for thatching roofs with Norfolk reeds. All next week I will be helping the thatcher complete a new home that is being built.

Master Snow is adding a lean-to on the back side of his house. This is a popular way of expanding a dwelling here.

We danced this afternoon. Hester Cooke lost the two ribbons attached to the back of her bodice and I found them.

It will probably rain soon as the frogs are croaking a lot tonight and soot has been falling down the chimney.

July 9, 1627

*W*hen today's outdoor meeting was held near the fields, I prayed that a ship never comes because I am happy here and do not wish to move to Jamestown. We also prayed that our crops will flourish.

Desire Howland's parents complained that their daughter should be baptized, as she is six months old. The Deacon explained that only a pastor can perform such a ceremony and

Plimoth does not have one residing here.

During the meeting, Mistress Warren fainted due to being out in the hot sun for so many hours. I fear the Mistress may be ailing as she looks thin and has poor color.

Godbert Godbertson's spaniel died from eating chicken bones that caught in its throat. It was an obedient and faithful dog.

July 11, 1627

*J*ohnathan is thinking about moving to Duxbury. John Alden and Myles Standish want lots there also, as they say they do not see a prosperous future in Plimoth. Master Brewster is distressed at the idea of being alone should Wrestling and Love follow.

There was little discussion after our evening meal.

July 14, 1627

*W*hen drilling this afternoon, Bartholomew and I added an extra beat to the march. This was unappreciated and we were promptly scolded.

I cut a quantity of herbs to dry for cooking, as well as calendula blossoms to color butter in the winter.

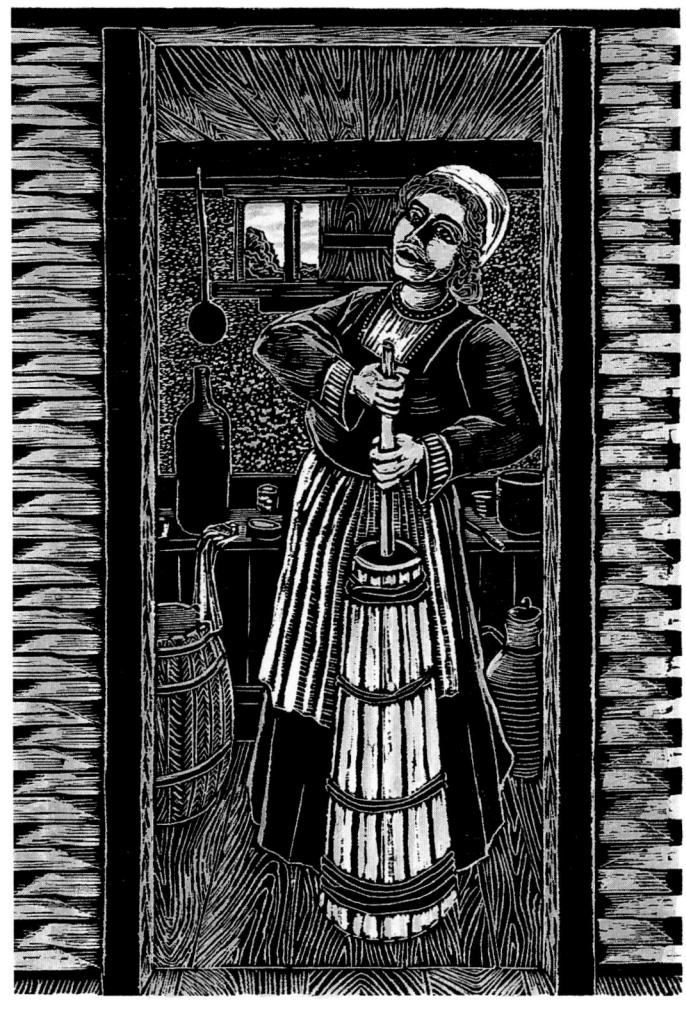

Elinor Adams recommends this chant when making butter:

> *Come butter come,*
> *Come butter come,*
> *Peter's at the gate*
> *And he wants a little butter cake.*

Elinor says this always makes the cream separate quickly, as long as the churn is not made with ash tree wood. She also suggested that this chant be kept as "a little secret from Master Brewster."

July 18, 1627

We have been gathering sassafras bark to export to England. It is worth two shillings a pound and makes a very good tea.

During this evening's lesson, Master Brewster spoke of his friendship with Thomas Weston, who promoted the Adventurers when they left Leiden, Holland, and later sailed over on the *Mayflower* from England. I did not know that ship was a rundown old wine vessel.

The Master also told me of the two persons who died during the voyage and how Francis Billington nearly blew up the *Mayflower* by playing around the powder stores as the ship rounded Cape Cod.

I may be in love with Humility Cooper, who was put to Thomas and Patience Prence. She is very intelligent. Humility gave me some candied flowers dipped in egg white and sugar.

July 21, 1627

There has been a terrible tragedy! John Alden's house just burned to the ground. We are all thankful that no one was injured. It is believed that a chink in the chimney filled with soot and caught fire.

We formed a bucket brigade from the spring to the Alden house. There was so much commotion and smoke in the air that I was reminded of life in London, where there was always excitement.

We tried to douse the blaze, but once the thatch ignited there was no chance of saving the structure. Most of the furnishings and their Bible were rescued.

The Aldens are going to stay with the Governor. It has been a frightful evening and I do not think it will be easy to fall asleep.

July 24, 1627

*L*ate last night when I went out to the ajax to relieve myself, John Crackstone was standing near the redoubt, staring at the sky.

It was amazing! There were large arches and streamers of pulsing colored light flashing across the heavens. John called it the "aurora borealis." If the sky is clear tonight, John says the phenomenon will probably be visible again.

Love wants to betroth Mary Warren, but he fears she may be fonder of Edward Bangs.

July 27, 1627

*W*e have been gathering wood, splitting and stacking it for winter use.

Love cleaned our chimney by firing a musket up inside the stack. This loosened all the soot. A few cracks needed to be filled with daub. Master Brewster says that the lining of the chimney should be repaired at least twice a year.

*I*t looks as though this season's crop of Indian corn will yield abundantly.

Master Brewster said that when the Adventurers first scouted the land along the Cape, they found a mound of sand that had been neatly patted by human hands. Inside were 36 ears of corn the natives had stored so they did not have to carry it with them. That seed saved the settlers from starving their first year here because Squanto taught them how to plant it and harvest the corn, which is the plantation's most important produce now.

Fear brought us some fresh bread and grape conserve.

August 9, 1627

*T*he Governor has asked Myles Standish, Johnathan, and me to journey to the Wampanoag settlement for fur trading with Chief Massasoit. His Worship wants me to illustrate how the Indians live and has made suggestions as to what details I should depict.

We will depart on our journey in two days. Master Brewster thinks I should leave my journal at home as the text could be damaged should there be foul weather.

August 18, 1627

*T*oday when we returned from the Indian settlement, I learned that two barks had arrived from Jamestown to transport the *Sparrowhawk* passengers to Virginia. For me it was not a welcome sight.

Master Brewster is going to try to purchase my indenture papers from Sibsey so I may remain here. Some of the other passengers have also chosen to stay.

August 19, 1627

*T*he sailors from Jamestown told us of the troubles they have had with Indians who massacred the settlement residents many times. Since 1607, nearly 10,000 people have sailed over to establish Jamestown. Only 2,000 have survived. The rest died due to illness and other events.

The residents also have black slaves that are captured in Africa and have been sold in

Jamestown since 1620 to work the farms. Master Brewster says slavery is abominable. In a way I am a slave myself to Captain Sibsey.

Sibsey says he will discuss the matter of my papers with the Master the day after tomorrow.

I may run away. Richard has said he will go with me and we can return after the barks have sailed.

August 20, 1627

The Sabbath meeting was declared a day of thanksgiving because of the safe arrival of the ships. The service was held in the fort. The birth of a baby boy to Stephen and Elizabeth Hopkins was announced and that is all I remember of the eight-hour service.

I went to Mistress Brewster's grave and said a prayer.

August 21, 1627

Sibsey has refused to sell my papers, but Master Brewster has told me not to despair because he will take the matter to a higher authority—the Governor.

The belongings of the *Sparrowhawk* passengers have been gathered in one place to estimate the amount of storage space needed to transport them. We were told to bring only necessities, which is all we were allowed to bring in the first place! Fells and Sibsey reminded us that we will be servants in established homes and will not need all the implements required to set up house-keeping. Sibsey said that I may not bring the blocks of wood that my pictures are carved on because "there will be plenty of kindling in Jamestown already." He had such a smug expression when he said it. I have never liked or respected Sibsey.

Richard and Love keep telling me not to give up hope and to say prayers.

August 22, 1627

The Governor met with Master Brewster and does not feel that he can legally force Sibsey to sign me over to the Master despite the circumstances that brought me here.

Since the ship will depart Thursday at sunrise, tomorrow will be my last full day here.

I feel very sad.

*M*y eyes are so filled with tears that it is difficult to write.

This evening the Brewsters and Fear and her children had a special farewell dinner in my honor. I even sat in Master Brewster's chair, which he said was reserved for important persons.

After a meal of all my favorite foods, Johnathan presented me with a new copy book to replace mine, which he knew to be nearly full. Dear Johnathan had bartered his ribbons with one of the sailors in exchange for it.

I tried to be cheerful and told them it was like having a double celebration because this was also my birthday. Master Brewster stood raising his glass and said, "Let us have a toast to our beloved Christopher's thirteenth year." When I corrected him and told them that today I am fourteen, Johnathan dropped his tankard, spilling its contents, and Master Brewster grabbed his hat and rushed out the door, saying he would be back shortly. I was confused.

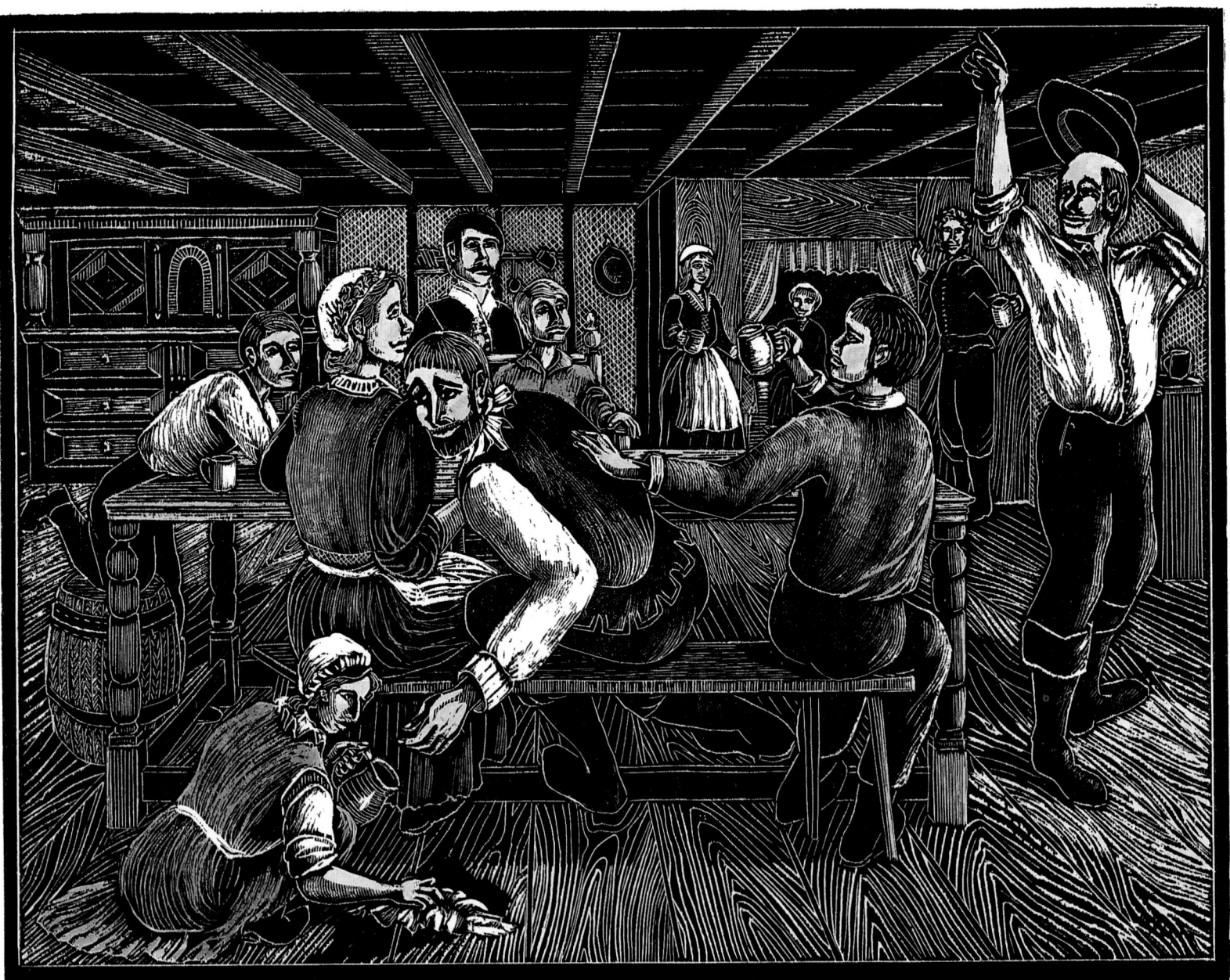

Johnathan whispered to Love and soon they all knew something that certainly lightened the atmosphere. It made me feel better just to see them laughing and smiling again.

Within the hour, Master Brewster burst back into the house with news that he had just talked with Governor Bradford and Sibsey. It seems that at the age of 14, an orphan can legally choose his own guardian and the Master convinced His Worship that I had clearly made my choice. As a result, the Governor forced Sibsey to release my indenture papers to Master Brewster!

The Master also said Governor Bradford wants me to know that he is pleased at the outcome of this matter as he was most disheartened at the thought of losing New England's first artist.

I have been rejoicing and merry-making with the Brewsters!

Tomorrow—soon as the ship is out of sight—I will begin another book. This text will be delivered to my grandparents first, and then to the King.

The woodcuts in this book were cut on cherry and pearwood, printed, and the resultant monochrome
proofs hand-colored with inks. Woodcuts were the most widely used—albeit the most difficult—method of making
multiple prints in the seventeenth century.

Stranded at Plimoth Plantation 1626
Copyright © 1994 by Gary Bowen
Introduction copyright © 1994 by HarperCollins Publishers Inc.

Library of Congress Cataloging-in-Publication Data
Bowen, Gary.
    Stranded at Plimoth Plantation 1626 / words and woodcuts by Gary Bowen ; introduction by
David Freeman Hawke.
        p.   cm.
    ISBN 0-06-022541-6. — ISBN 0-06-022542-4 (lib. bdg.) — ISBN 0-06-440719-5 (pbk.)
    1. Pilgrims (New Plymouth Colony)—Juvenile literature   2. Massachusetts—Social life and customs—
To 1775—Juvenile literature. 3. Massachusetts—History—New Plymouth, 1620–1691—Juvenile litera-
ture. [1. Pilgrims (New Plymouth Colony).   2. Massachusetts—Social life and customs—To 1775.
3. Massachusetts—History—New Plymouth, 1620–1691.] I. Title.
F68.B742   1994   93-31016
973.2'1—dc20   CIP
                                                                                             AC

Typography by Tom Starace
❖
Visit us on the World Wide Web!
http://www.harperchildrens.com